FRIENDS

Written by

Catherine Thimmesh

HOUGHTON MIFFLIN • HOUGHTON MIFFLIN HARCOURT • BOSTON NEW YORK

Houghton Mifflin is an imprint of Houghton Mifflin Harcourt Publishing Company.

www.hmhbooks.com

The text of this book is set in ITC Usherwood.

Library of Congress Cataloging-in-Publication Control Number 2010025122

ISBN 978-0-547-39010-9

Manufactured in China

LEO 10 9 8 7 6 5 4

4500326554

PHOTO CREDITS:

macaque/pigeon (p. 5): Huojb/Photoshot

orangutan/cat (p. 7): Stephanie Willard/Zoo World

camel/pig (p. 9): Ilya Naymushin/Reuters

giraffe/ostrich (p. 11): Matt Marriott/Busch Gardens Tampa Bay/Press Association via AP Images

lion cub/piglet (p. 13): Liezl Swanepoel/Harnas African Wildlife Rescue

basset hound/owl (p. 14): Katharyn Boudet

frog/mouse (p. 17): Pawan Kumar/Reuters

fox/badger (pp. 1, 19): Peter Corns/Genset Pictures

capybara/monkey (pp. 2, 21): Kim Hyung Hoon/Reuters

polar bear/dog (both images) (pp. 22, 32): Norbert Rosing/Photoshot

black bear/cat (p. 25): Karl Bröseke/Zoological Garden Berlin

cheetah/dog (both images) (pp. 3, 27): Barry Bland

baby orangutan/tiger (hugging) (p.29): Dimas Ardian/Getty Images

baby orangutan/tiger (looking at each other) (p. 30): Achmad Ibrahim/AP Photos

For my favorite young friends (the nephews & nieces):
Noah, Isaac, and Theodore
Andy and Sam
Julianna, Angelina, John, and Alexandra

A special thanks to animal lovers Noah and Ike, who
helped me preview the pictures

A friend comforts . . .

A pat,
a hug,
and a new friend is made;
no longer alone,
no longer afraid.

An abandoned baby macaque was nursed back to health at an animal rescue hospital on Neilingding Island in China. But the macaque still appeared sad and forlorn, showing none of the species' usual zest or playfulness. That is, until he crossed paths with a pigeon—and gave it a hug. It's not known if macaque and pigeon were together for several days or several months. But at least for a time, each seemed to find comfort in the other.

No matter
if one walks
on four legs
or two—
a friend provides comfort
when one's feeling blue.

When the old orangutan at Zoo World in Florida lost her mate, she was listless and would barely eat. Workers worried that she might very well lose her will to live. So they brought a new companion— a stray tabby cat—to her enclosure; first just outside the fence, then in. The two became instant and inseparable friends. For nearly four years, Tonda the orangutan and TK the cat lived side by side— eating, playing, sleeping—until Tonda died of old age. But for four years, both were comforted and

A friend connects . . .

A stretch,
a slight strain,
a balancing feat;
friends go to great lengths
in order to meet.

t the Roev Ruchey Zoo in Siberia, there is a simple fence that separates the Asian camels from th

ietnamese miniature pigs. But one day, one of the camels thrust her curvy neck over and dowr

hile the pig pushed up on squat hind legs . . . both curious to see what was on the other side. Fc

eeks, for months—even still today—Ldinka the camel and Pashka the pig reached out to eac

ther to connect and be close. They relax together too, nuzzled up side by side with only the woode

lanks of a fence between them.

No matter
who has
a snout
or a beak,
connecting with friends
is something friends seek.

trich and giraffe both roam the sprawling sixty-five-acre Serengeti exhibit at Busch Ga

pa Bay, Florida. One day, the spirited young giraffe swooped her long neck downward

d her sticky tongue on the old ostrich, exploring. Rather than running away, the ostrich

hough it's not clear how much or how often they interact, Bea the giraffe and Wilma the c

ind up a bit sticky whenever they're together.

A friend snuggles . . .

A nestle,
a nuzzle,
a much-needed squeeze;
friends rest together—
completely at ease.

One day at the Harnas African Wildlife Rescue in Namibia, a lazy-feeling lion cub sprawled out in the dirt. A piglet stumbled upon him. Both of them happened to be in the same place at the same time, and both were rather sleepy. Every day, Brad the lion and Wilbur the pig would nap and play together. But the lion's growing size and strength posed a danger—a grown lion would oftentimes eat a pig. Still, for six months, before the two had to be separated, lion and pig snuggled up

No matter
if covered
in fur
or feather,
friends are calm and relaxed
when snuggled together.

At an animal rescue home in Tenterdon, Kent, England, a hurt basset hound lounged in the living room, sprawled in front of the TV screen. One day, a tawny owl decided to investigate—drawn to the flickering images, or maybe the floppy ears. He plunked down right next to the dog. The droopy-eyed dog didn't bother to move. And so for five years (and counting), Beryl the hound and Wol the owl met together on the couch. And snuggled.

A friend helps . . .

A boost,
a lift,
a ride piggyback;
a friend is someone
who picks up the slack.

Monsoon waters filled the streets in Lucknow, India, flooding the city with destruction and death. This plucky mouse, however, caught a ride on a passing frog, and—with tiny claws clutching craggy skin—navigated the floodwaters to safety. Most likely, frog and mouse weren't buddies for long. The frog was just willing to help out in a crisis.

No matter
if eyes
are black
or gold,
friends help each other
when sadness takes hold.

This baby badger and baby fox arrived at the Warwickshire Wildlife Sanctuary in England (a week

apart) quite ill. In time, they gained strength and energy, but their days were dull and dreary and

sad. Until one day they started running and tumbling along side by side, helping each other to

spend their bottled-up energy. They enjoyed their days together for four months, until the fox died of

health problems. It was such an unlikely relationship, the sanctuary decided to photograph it. They

placed Lulu (the fox) and Humbug (the badger) in front of a backdrop. The animals nudged close

A friend plays . . .

A leap,
a plop,
and the game begins;
a friend won't mind
which one of them wins.

Officials at the Tobu Zoo in Japan had only one space to house two different species. The capy-baras, the world's largest rodents, would have the grounds near the water; and the teensy two-pound squirrel monkeys would scamper above in the branches. This is exactly how they would live in their native rainforest—never interacting. But then one day, a mischievous monkey landed with a purposeful plop right onto a capy's back! And the mild-mannered capy didn't complain. A game was invented, and for months (and still today), capybara and squirrel monkey played and played and played.

No matter
who's small,
or who weighs
a ton—
friends romp and they roll
and their day turns to fun.

On the frozen tundra of Manitoba, Canada, a twelve-hundred-pound polar bear approached some chained Eskimo sled dogs. The photographer on site was certain the bear would eat a dog—or two. But surprisingly, despite his aggressive instincts, this polar bear just wanted to play. He buddied up to one of the dogs and together they wrestled and played through the evening. For ten straight days, the polar bear came back and frolicked with the sled dog until sundown. Then, the bear was gone.

A friend protects . . .

A snarl
a swat,
an aggressive display—
a friend keeps the other
out of harm's way.

At nighttime, a big Asiatic bear slept at the Berlin Zoo, blending into the blackness. But while the bear

snoozed, a not-so-big cat snooped around, and somehow crawled right into the bear's enclosure. For

reasons unknown, Maüschen the bear didn't attack. Inexplicably, she also protected Müschi the cat

from the other Asiatic bears. And that night—and for twelve years now—the small ball of charcoal-

colored fluff snuggled down deep, surrounded by the protective paws of a great big bear.

if spotted
or dot-less and white,
a friend gives protection
through day and through night.

At the Cincinnati Zoo in Ohio, a cheetah cub and Antolian pup were brought together to play. They chased and wrestled and chewed on each other. The two soon became inseparable: eating and playing and sleeping side by side. They traveled with zoo staff to schools and events, keeping audiences engaged as workers explained a program about protecting cheetahs in the African wild using Antolian guard dogs. For more than eight years now, Sahara the cheetah and Alexa the dog have been friends. Now they each prefer their own space to live in, but whenever they come together for a zoo program on cheetah protection, they lick each other hello.

Friends . . .

Friends can be different—
with stripes on their face;
or friends can have
fingers
to touch and embrace . . .

but it doesn't matter—
not in the end—
because deep where it counts,
one knows a true friend.

Orphans at the Taman Safari Zoo in Bogor, Indonesia, this baby orangutan and Sumatran tiger cub didn't know they were supposed to be enemies. (In the wild, grown tigers will eat orangutans.) One day, in the zoo nursery, the orangutan gently groomed the tiger's scruffy neck, and the cub playfully slurped the orangutan's long fingers. For months, they played nonstop—and grew nonstop. Then the zoo staff had to separate them, for their own safety. But during those months, they wrestled and rolled and romped. And once worn out, Dema the tiger cub and Nia the orangutan settled down together . . . and cuddled in close.

Acknowledgments

A very special thanks and my enormous gratitude goes out to the many talented photographers who were there at just the right time and able to capture the truth and beauty inherent in these unlikely, but very real, animal friendships.

Thanks to the photographers:

Huojb, Stephanie Willard, Ilya Naymushin, Matt Marriott, Liezl Swanepoel, Katharyn Boudet, Pawan Kumar, Peter Corns, Kim Hyung Hoon, Norbert Rosing, Karl Bröseke, Barry Bland, Dimas Ardian, and Achmad Ibrahim

and to

Kris Hook, Photoshot; Nancy Glowinski, Thomson Reuters; Carolyn McGoldrick, AP Photos; Brian Blankenburg, Getty Images; Catherine Leon, Harnas African Wildlife Rescue; Elizabeth Bassler and Jason Green, Busch Gardens Tampa Bay; Regine Damm, Berlin Zoo; Stacey Clark, Warwickshire Wildlife Sanctuary; and Linda Castaneda, Cincinnati Zoo.

Zoo World: www.zooworldpcb.net
Busch Gardens Tampa Bay: www.buschgardens.com/Bgt/default.aspx
Harnas African Wildlife Rescue: www.harnasusa.org
Warwickshire Wildlife Sanctuary: www.warwickshirewildlifesanctuary.co.uk
Berlin Zoo: www.zoo-berlin.de/en.html
Taman Safari Zoo: www.tamansafari.com
Cincinnati Zoo: www.cincinnatizoo.org
cheetah protection/conservation program: www.cheetah.co.za/news_shadow.html
Katharyn Boudet, photographer: www.katzeye.co.uk
Norbert Rosing, photographer: www.rosing.de

And, of course, a heartfelt thanks to the wonderful Ann Rider.